Ugh! Eggs!

Sarah Arnold

Dad cooked eggs
for breakfast.

Pip hates eggs!

Pip was very hungry,
so he went to see his Aunt Nellie.

Aunt Nellie went straight
to the kitchen...

...and made him
a huge pile of sandwiches.

He looked inside...

"Ugh! Eggs!"

While Aunt Nellie made
herself a cup of tea,

He fed one
to the bird.

Pip stuffed two sandwiches
between the cushions.

He put two in his pocket...

...and he squashed one into the vase.

He threw one
out of the window.

He placed two under the rug.

He slipped one under
the couch, and he locked
two in the cupboard.

Aunt Nellie came back
into the room.

"My, you were hungry! I can't believe you've eaten all my egg sandwiches!"

"Now, do you have room for something else?"

"Shall we make a cake?"

Into Aunt Nellie's
cake went...

1 cup of sugar

2 drops of vanilla essence

1 cup of very soft butter

1 cup of flour

1 teaspoon of baking powder…

...and two...

Now poor Pip was ravenous.
He scooted through the woods
with a grumbling, empty stomach,
feeling quite miserable.

But as he turned the corner,
there was a familiar smell.

A lovely smell!

He followed his nose,
scooting faster and faster,
until he reached...

...his dad's kitchen.

There on the table, was a big, warm, freshly-baked cake.

It was...

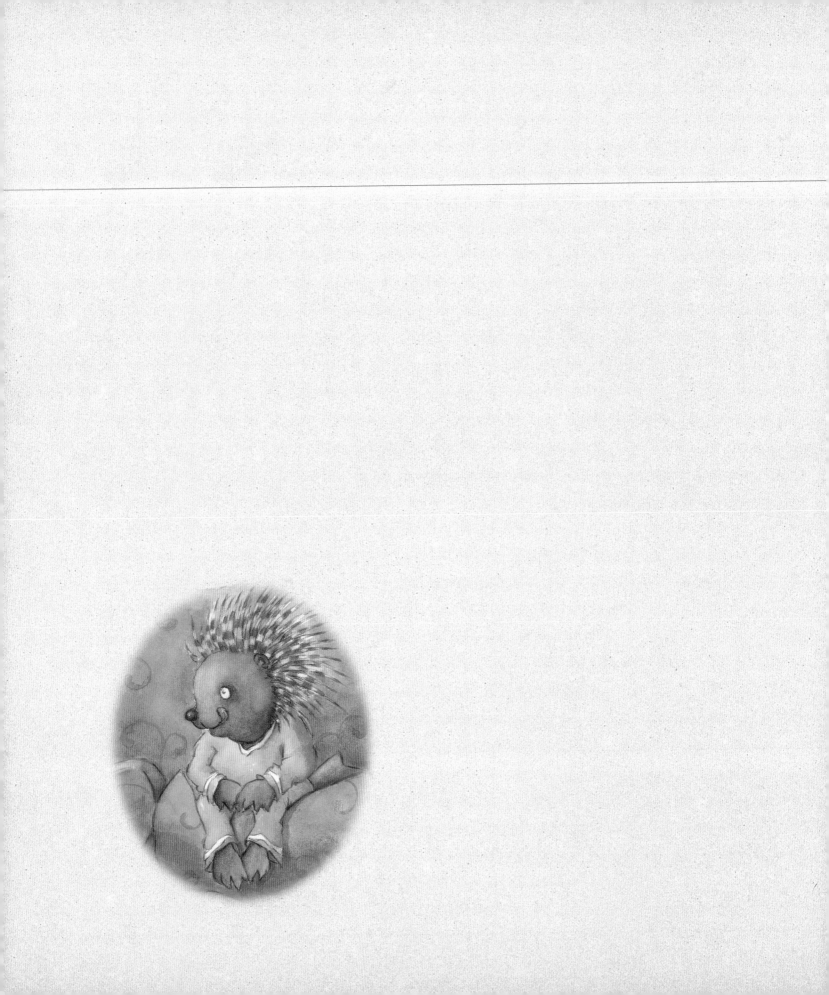

First published in 2010
by Child's Play (International) Ltd
Ashworth Road, Bridgemead,
Swindon SN5 7YD

Distributed in USA by Child's Play Inc
250 Minot Avenue, Auburn, Maine 04210

Distributed in Australia by Child's Play Australia Pty Ltd
Unit 10/20 Narabang Way, Belrose, NSW 2085

ISBN 978-1-84643-342-9
CLP020610CPL09103429

Printed and bound in Shenzhen, China   1   3   5   7   9   10   8   6   4   2

A catalogue record of this book is available from the British Library   www.childs-play.com